Professor Odd #2

Other Heliopause Productions:

THE ADVENTURES OF BOURAGNER FELPZ
Volume I: A Study of Magic

APSIS FICTION
The Semi-Annual Anthology of Goldeen Ogawa
Volume 1, No. 1: Mesohelion 2013

PROFESSOR ODD
#1 The False Student
#2 The Slowly Dying Planet

Coming Soon:

#3 The Promethean Predicament

heliopauseweb.com

PROFESSOR ODD
THE SLOWLY DYING PLANET

Professor Odd #2

by

GOLDEEN OGAWA

a Heliopause Production

For information contact Heliopause Productions at
www.heliopauseweb.com.

FICTION/Science Fiction, Adventure

PROFESSOR ODD: THE SLOWLY DYING PLANET was first published as an e-book in 2011 by Goldeen Ogawa.

First Print Edition 2013

ISBN: 978-1-4929726-6-2

Prologue

It was always night outside Alister's window. At least, it appeared that way. When he sat up in bed and drew aside the lace-trimmed shades all he saw was a deep, bluish darkness pricked with what looked like countless stars.

But they were not stars, as the Professor had explained to him at length; they were *worlds.* Entire universes, each with their own infinite set of possibilities and parallel dimensions, floating in a sea of nothing. Sometimes one would drift close enough that Alister could make out individual stars and planets within the glowing sphere that surrounded them. Sometimes all he could see was one world, with continents and clouds, even tiny cities. When he had asked about this the Professor had explained that the spheres were not the universes themselves, merely pinprick windows into them. What you saw on the other side depended on where the pinprick was.

And—this was what truly boggled his mind—the Professor had visited many of them. She could recognize several, and even pointed out his own: a faint swirl of blue-green light at the end of a string of similar lights. It made him feel small and lonely, seeing his entire world as a pinprick in that vast black emptiness.

The only other thing out there, besides the eternal night and the points of light, was the Oddity.

Alister got out of bed. He was hungry, which was how they measured days and nights in the Oddity. He still wasn't sure if it was ship or a house, but he didn't bother asking; its name explained it as well as anyone could, and Alister accepted what it did (opening doors to other universes) as a matter of fact. He had to, otherwise his neat, rational brain would probably explode.

Alister got dressed. The Oddity had provided him with a pair of striped pajamas and a selection of brightly colored shirts, trousers and drawers. Alister wore the drawers (because he had to) and the shirts (because his own smelled funny), but he stubbornly clung to his own pair of sensible trousers and conservative brown jacket. After three days of consecutive wear these were beginning to wrinkle, but Alister was damned if he would be seen in neon-pink jeans with yellow stars blazoned across the back pockets. Even if he would only be seen by three people.

Well, two people . . . and a tentacle monster.

Alister's room was on the second level of the Oddity, and his door opened onto a catwalk that ran around the inside of the place in a giant tear-drop shape. A trap-ladder led down to the lower level, which served as a living room, study, kitchen, dining room, and (in the narrow end of the teardrop) cockpit. On his way to the ladder Alister passed three doors, each made of painted white wood with a brass handle, but individually decorated. The first had a symbol like a green sun with ten rays shining out of it; this room belonged to Dave, and the door was cracked ajar, letting out ominous scrapings and high-pitched whining sounds of metal being welded together. Dave was building himself an all-environment mobility suit, since the Oddity's natural climate—that of a 22° Celsius nitrogen-oxygen atmosphere—tended to dry him out.

The second door was somewhat battered and looked older than the first. It had a large sign nailed to it that declared "Beware of the Dog" in sharp red letters. Only "Dog" had been crossed out and someone had written *"Vroknaär"* underneath it in careful cursive. This room belonged to Elo. Alister had asked her what a *vroknaär* was. She had told him it was to a wolf what a human was to an *australopithecus.*

The last door looked like it had been repainted several times, each time with a different color. Currently it was a refreshing mint green, but showed traces of orange and yellow through the cracks. It clashed rather with the dull salmon wallpaper, and its only decoration was a metal "0-D" (of the sort used to mark street addresses) bolted to the center. This was the Professor's room, and Alister had never seen the inside of it.

There was a fourth room, just beyond the ladder, that held a sign with a pictograph for a male and female character, a dog, and the ten-rayed sun symbol. This was the bathroom, and Alister took advantage of it before descending the ladder.

Elo emerged from the kitchen alcove just as Alister reached the floor. She was wearing a rumpled apron over her purple jumpsuit, and her ears were drooping sadly.

"We're out of food," she declared, and flopped down at the table.

Alister's stomach chose that time to grumble loudly.

"Are you sure?" he said. "Absolutely out?"

Elo wrinkled her nose. "Well, there's half a bag of broccoli, but *that* doesn't *count.*"

Alister had to admit that, even to his omnivorous tastes, broccoli was not what he wanted for breakfast. He went and joined Elo at the table, carefully clearing himself a space among the pile of junk and oddments that decorated it. Along at the far end of the table, where half a bicycle had been propped up against an ebony safe marked with a skull and crossbones, a disheveled figure in an olive green trench coat and a bright blue wig shuddered to life. It rubbed its face with a pair of long white hands, and blinked at them out of golden cat eyes.

"Did someone say *food?*" Professor Odd asked.

"Out," Elo snapped. "I said we're *out* of food."

The Professor groaned and laid her head on the table. A moment later she popped it up again, her eyes bright and a wide grin on her face.

"Pizza," she said.

"Sorry?" said Alister.

"I want *pizza!*" cried the Professor. "After twelve hours of programming Dave's infernal nano-bots, I need *pizza!* Dave!" she called, standing up and bellowing at the half-open door with the green sun on it. "We're going to get pizza, are you coming?"

The clanging from within the other room ceased. The door creaked as it swung the rest of the way open, and a long green tentacle emerged. It was dripping with pale green slime, and was coiled around an allen wrench. It seemed puzzled. Then it retreated, and emerged again with the rest of its body: a disc the size and shape of a pie plate, with one round yellow-and-orange eye in the center. Two more tentacles held a small black box with a speaker mounted to it against the creature's underside.

"I HAVE EATEN ONE HUNDRED HOURS AGO." Dave intoned through the machine. "I SHALL NOT REQUIRE NUTRIENTS FOR ANOTHER HUNDRED AT MINIMUM." He paused and fiddled with the machine. "I HAVE WORK TO PERFORM. BRING ME BACK YOUR LEFTOVERS." And with a flick of tentacle, he was gone.

"Well," said the Professor, beaming at them. "Just us three, then?"

The cockpit at the narrow end of the Oddity was a jumble of lights, screens, buttons and levers. Alister could not make sense of it. He did not *want* to make sense of it. The only thing he could understand was the door, set at the bottom of a flight of stairs between the pilot chairs, that was currently a black slab of nothing. That door could lead anywhere, any place, in any universe. But *how* it did it, he had no idea.

Professor Odd swung herself into a chair and caused the display in front of her to light up with a pleased humming sound. Elo got into the other chair and craned her neck around to look at the Professor.

"Where are we going for pizza?" she asked. "Napoli?"

"Oh no," said the Professor, punching at the buttons before her. "Pizza Margherita is far too heavy for my taste. Think farther afield."

"New York?" Alister hazarded. "Maybe Chicago?"

Professor Odd laughed. "Farther than that, my friend!" she cried, and flipped the red lever at her right hand.

It was like watching a fireworks display, only without the bangs. The lights in the cockpit glittered and pulsed, settling into a pattern that traced its way from the Professor's console to Elo's, and as each button or bulb flashed, it hummed. The large beacons set into the supporting columns buzzed. The smaller lights pinged. The fiber optic cables sang. A string of tiny bulbs guided a single white spark up a column where it crashed into a giant sphere like a golden disco ball which clanged like a gong. Then all the lights spiraled, concentrating on the black rectangle of the door. At the peak of the crescendo of light and sound the doorway itself flashed white and gave off a single, pure note which hung in the air even as the lights and other sounds died away.

Where the black rectangle had been, there was now a stone archway with a flimsy wooden door.

Elo was busy tapping away at her rack of buttons as the Professor grabbed her scarf from the table and tied it around her neck.

"Simple precautions," Elo explained when Alister leaned over her shoulder. "I'm setting the Oddity to recognize only our narrative stamp, so that it won't accidentally kidnap some poor old native."

"Has that happened before?" Alister asked.

"Oh yes," Elo said. "How do you think I got here?"

"Right then, ready to go?" Professor Odd said. She had buttoned up her trench coat and was carrying her black walking cane with the silver banana handle. All in all she looked rather dapper, if someone wearing red pinstriped trousers, a drab olive coat, and a blue wig could be said to look dapper. Alister noticed that her dark glasses, which usually hid her eyes, had been left off.

"Your glasses," he began, picking up his everything bag.

"Won't make a difference on this world," she said, waving a hand dismissively. She strode down the stairs, followed closely by Elo, who had taken off her apron at the last minute and stuffed it under her chair.

The Professor opened the door and stood aside. "There you are," she said. "After you."

Alister emerged from the Oddity to find himself in a narrow, stone-cobbled street. Looking around he saw all the buildings were of stone, with wooden doors and lights set under the eaves. In the distance he could hear the rumble of traffic and the clank and hiss of some steam-powered machine. At first he thought it must be sunset, because the light was the rich, warm orange he always associated with sunsets, and it was much dimmer. Then he looked up.

I'm on an alien planet! was the first thing through his mind.

The sky was wrong. It was the wrong color, for a start: a deep, rich orange, streaked with red clouds. This was a little unnerving, but what made him gasp, what made him stand frozen, staring at the southern horizon, was the arching crescent that rose up halfway to where the sun (somehow redder and gentler than it should be) hung in the burnished sky.

Alister had seen pictures of planets in his astronomy class. Most of them had been illustrative, and had shown the planet as a perfect sphere. But there had been others that showed the planet partly lit, so that it melted into the blackness of space and only a narrow crescent could be seen. This was what Alister saw in the southern sky. If he had been capable at that moment of making words, and then using those words to describe what he saw, he would have said it looked like the planet Jupiter turned greenish, and very, very close.

Professor Odd smiled and put an arm around her stricken companion. "Welcome to Niatano, Mister Alister," she said, smiling proudly up at the gas giant, as if she had put it there and were admiring her handiwork.

Something tore the sky in half.

It was white and deafening, and knocked Elo to all fours and Alister and the Professor against the stone building behind them. Below the thunderous roar came the delicate screaming of breaking glass and the sudden angry honking of vehicle horns and the screech of brakes. A shower of rock dust fell from the high roofs above their heads, and the building groaned ominously.

Wiping dust out of his eyes Alister blinked up at the sky, now bisected by an angry tumult of frothing clouds. He felt the iron grip of the Professor's hand on his shoulder, and when he turned to look saw that she too was staring up at the sky. But not with fear or confusion. The expression on the Professor's face was of cold, resigned fury.

"That!" she exclaimed. "That! *That!* That was *not* supposed to happen!"

Part One

IN CONTROL ROOMS all over the world, chaos was breaking out. It was the near-panicked, yet purposeful chaos of people who have important things to do, even if they didn't know exactly what—and even though these people might not have been recognizable *as* people at first glance.

In the control room at the top of the tallest skyscraper, in the city where the Professor had just appeared, orders were shouted—but not in English. More rushing about, tails flying dangerously close to expensive computer banks, and one character in a bright red uniform caused the display covering half the wall to show an aerial view of a smoking crater. Around the edges were what looked like ruins of a city, and pale yellow tongues of flame were licking their way over the smoking rubble.

Cries of dismay and anguish arose from the occupants of the room. One collapsed onto a chair-like object, holding his head in his hands and whispering, *"No, no, non Caprisio . . . "*

Only one character was not affected by the disaster. She sat in a corner in front of a smaller bank of monitors which showed, in grainy black and white, different angles of a back alley somewhere in that very city. In the alley were three unusual—at least to her bright yellow eyes—creatures, one of which appeared to be a sort of canine. Typing in more commands on the rack of keys in front of her, she brought up the coordinates of that alley. Satisfied, she rolled her chair-thing back and stood up, raising her long tail for balance.

She grabbed a passing redcoat, and injected some orders into his ear-frill. Reluctantly he allowed himself to be dragged out of the control room, taking a projectile weapon from the rack just outside the door, and together they trotted down the hall to a door marked with the multiuniversal sign for an elevator.

* * *

In the alley Professor Odd had whipped out a compass, growled, put it back, then whipped out a *different* compass, and was now triangulating the trajectory of the trail of white cloud while Elo jotted down the results. Alister, left with nothing to do but wait while the initial thrill of adrenaline subsided, followed by a mild tinge of queasiness, which was eventually shouldered aside by his pervasive hunger, began to wander. He got as far as the end of the alley, where he poked his head around the corner, and saw what looked like two small dinosaurs in police uniforms running towards him.

Ducking back into the alley he sprinted over to the Professor and tapped her elbow. "I think we've been spotted," he told her urgently.

"Eh?" said the Professor, looking up from her compass. "Well, of course we would, with something like *that* this whole place is going to be ringing with surveillance."

"Professor," Elo said sharply, her ears perking, "they are up-wind of us; they are very scared."

"Yes, and running this way," Alister added. "I think they are *police.*"

"What color are their uniforms?" the Professor asked, pocketing her compass.

"Er, one is red, I think," Alister said. "The other's a sort of orange-brown."

"Oh!" Professor Odd exclaimed with a smile. "Then we should be all right." And she turned down the alley, where the two creatures had just wheeled into view. "Ah!" she said, as if greeting old friends. *"Ciao, ciao,"* and then tumbled out a torrent of speech in what Alister recognized, a little incredulously, as *Italian.*

The creatures were similarly affected. One—the one in red—lowered the projectile weapon to its side and looked at its companion, who had folded its arms across its chest and was regarding the Professor with unmistakable skepticism.

They did not look so much like dinosaurs after all, Alister decided. Rather, they looked like a pair of oviraptors that had stood up, winched in their ostrich-like necks, grown shoulders, and sprouted each a crown of feathers from its head. Another tuft of feathers decorated the tip of each tail. One—the one in the orange-brown coat with gold buttons—had a head of dark feathers that extended over its neck, making it resemble a gaudy woman with an ostrich-feather boa wrapped around her throat.

Their faces were not human faces, yet they still managed to express recognizably human emotions. They had eyebrows in the form of ridges of dark scales that ran over and around the outer sides of their eyes, culminating in hook shapes over their upper cheeks. They had narrow, flat noses, and when they spoke their mouths were dark, for they had no teeth, only a pair of flat incisors, like a bird's beak. Their eyes were slanted and dark, and gleamed in the dim red light against rough, pale skin. Upon closer inspection Alister saw that the rough skin was not skin at all, but fine interlocking scales.

The feathery one in orange-brown, who seemed to be in charge, took out a small handheld device and began to manipulate its touch screen with its hands—hands that were recognizable as such even though they had three fingers and two thumbs.

The device bleeped at the creature, who looked from the readout to the Professor, then back again. It looked at its partner in apparent astonishment.

"*Si,*" it said in a light, husky voice. *"Questo é la Professoressa."* Then it put the device away, reached out its strange hand and shook Professor Odd's.

"I don't understand," Alister whispered fiercely at Professor Odd. "What *are* they?"

The two creatures were leading them at a near run through the narrow streets of the town, toward a white structure that looked like the Eiffel Tower, if the Eiffel Tower were an actual building with floors and windows and walls, not just a framework.

"They are *Ufficiale* Maria Rozione and Pierro," Professor Odd said. "They are *Umanitá;* but I call them Neätans. Helps avoid confusion, since *Umanitá* is just their word for *humanity.* Don't look so stricken: we aren't under arrest. Well, not yet. Maria is a *Carabinieri* knight, and they are generally pretty civilized."

"But, why are they *Italian?*"

"Strictly speaking they're *not* Italian," Elo interjected. "They are *Puchesi* . . . this *is* Pucca, isn't it Professor?"

Professor Odd was looking around at the houses as they passed; all of their windows were shuttered, and there was no one on the street besides themselves. They crossed a square that showed all the signs of having recently been a bustling marketplace, but was now eerily deserted: stalls had been abandoned with wares still on display; dropped goods and squashed packages of food littered the stone street.

"It was *supposed* to be," she said, her cat eyes narrowing. She walked faster, threatening to tread on Pierro's drooping tail. She began to speak—peppering the Neätans with questions—but in Italian, and Alister quickly gave up trying to follow the conversation.

The tower-like building stepped into view from around the front of a cathedral that was a little uphill of what could be considered Gothic: in place of a bell tower the cathedral had a slowly rotating Archimedes screw, on whose blade rode a golden orb, and its dome was split down the center, like the dome of an observatory. As they hurried past, Alister noticed that the stained-glass windows on the front showed strange stellar constellations, and the front doors were engraved with geometric proofs.

Then they were at the base of the tower, and *Ufficiale* Rozione was entering a security code on another touch-screen, while at the same time trying to answer the Professor's questions. These answers consisted of a lot of *"No"*s and a few *"Si!"*s. Professor Odd grew more impatient at each one.

Somewhere inside the building a latch released, and *Ufficiale* Rozione pushed open a door made of carved wood and cast iron, leading them into a passage with peeling wallpaper. Here things went suddenly, achingly ordinary: the smell of an old, lived-in building, the wear on the floor down the center of the hall. They passed a flight of stone stairs whose steps were so old they swayed in the middle like the back of a horse, and then crowded into an elevator that would have comfortably held four humans, but because of the Neätans' tails it became quite cramped. Alister wedged himself in a corner and tried to ignore the whining and creaking coming from above.

Professor Odd began speaking as soon as the doors were shut.

"It is *not* a self-inflicted attack," she explained, for the benefit of Alister and Elo. "They don't know *where* it came from, precisely, but they think it has something to do with a strange satellite they acquired about an hour ago . . . five minutes before that projectile was launched. They can't get an accurate image of the thing—it's jamming all their instruments—and there has been no communication from it."

"So, what is it?" Alister asked.

"I have no idea!" Professor Odd said. She sounded delighted. The Neätan's gave her strange looks; Alister noted that the scaly ridges above their eyes worked just like eyebrows, and that those eyes had dark sclera.

With a sound like a church bell the elevator came to a halt. Rozione got out first, nearly knocking Elo over with her tail, and made some sort of announcement in her native language. Then she beckoned them to follow her.

The Professor, Alister and Elo emerged into a scene of barely controlled chaos; about a dozen Neätans of every size and color—some short and squat, some long and lizard-like—inhabited a room already crowded with monitors, cables, and stacks of metal boxes decorated with blinking lights and fan vents.

For a brief moment they were stared at by twelve pairs of greenish-yellow alien eyes; frills were raised and lowered, scale-brows went up and down.

Then the room erupted in questions. Alister needed no translator to figure out what these were: "What are these things?" "Where did you find them?" "What is that strange, yellow, furry one?" And, most distressingly: "Are they responsible for our current problem?" This last was asked angrily by a stocky Neätan in a black uniform with red head-feathers cropped close to his skull.

Rozione attempted to field these questions as best she could, but when the redhead approached, Professor Odd swooped in and began speaking very fast, with lots of hand-gestures that Alister found bewildering, but the redhead seemed to follow. Slowly the stumps of his head-feathers settled, and he even lost a few inches as he levered his upper half down, counterbalanced by his tail. Alister wondered how he managed not to let that tail tangle in the cables that ran everywhere and draped in bundles from the ceiling.

With a hearty cry the redhead threw out his arms and embraced Professor Odd, who laughed as well.

"See, *this* is how you treat extra-universal travelers," she said, once the redhead had released her. "No locking them up in dungeons for experimentations—oh, I love Niatano! Now, who's trying to *destroy* it?"

"Destroy it?" Alister exclaimed. "You mean the *planet* is under attack?"

"Well, I did say that missile was not self-inflicted. And the bomb's explosion was powerful enough to have aftershocks felt 3,000 miles away . . . I'd say they pretty much mean—"

She was cut off as a number of alarms went off at once, and on the largest monitor a window popped into existence showing splotches of green and black, with a big orange bull's-eye blinking over an area speckled with white lights.

"Terrante! Terrante!" shouted a Neätan in brown over by the console. *"Loro hanno preso di mira Terrante!"*

"Merda!" grunted the redhead in black, then got a look of embarrassment on his face, and he rushed over to the console muttering, *"Prego, mi scusi . . . "*

This new crisis served to distract everyone in the room; in a stampede of brown and red uniforms and trailing tails all the Neätans clustered around this big screen, leaving the Professor, Alister and Elo in relative peace—except for *Ufficiale* Rozione, who remained dutifully by their side.

"I don't understand, what's *Terrante?*" Elo said.

Maria Rozione looked from the monitor, where their redheaded friend was delivering a torrent of Italian into a communication device, then down at her hands.

Professor Odd went over to a nearby console, which was scrolling white type on a black screen. The text, Alister noted in a distant way, was not unlike the Roman alphabet, save a few characters that were backwards or upside-down. The Russian one, then?

"*Terrante* is a city," Professor Odd said quietly, "that isn't going to be around for much longer."

Over by the largest screen, the redheaded Neätan was screeching into his communicator: *"Evacuare! Evacuare!"*

The steady beeping of the alarm by the console, which Alister had just begun to tune out, ratcheted up in pitch and volume, until it became a deafening wail—and just when he thought he couldn't stand anymore, it abruptly cut out.

There was silence in the control room. On the largest monitor a warning had come up. In the unnatural calm, Alister noticed that the Neätans also used the black exclamation point inside a yellow triangle to indicate trouble.

A few moments later they became aware of the growing rumble from outside the building, and a moment after that the floor shook beneath their feet. All the Neätans—and Elo—dropped to the ground; Alister grabbed at the nearest solid object.

Professor Odd rode out the tremors like a skateboarder going down a flight of stairs, and before they had quite subsided she marched over to the main console, pulling Neätans off the controls.

"Lasciami, per favore," she said, gently prying a sobbing Neätan off a keyboard. With a few quick strokes she dispatched the warnings and began pulling up readings—Alister was too far away to read them, but from the numerical figures that he could recognize he guessed they were coordinates.

"If I can just reverse-engineer the trajectory, maybe I can get an idea of their orbit," she was muttering when Alister arrived, stumbling over tails and cable bundles.

"What just happened there?" he demanded, though there was a sinking feeling in his gut that told him he already knew.

For answer the Professor jabbed her thumb at the screen next to hers, which, instead of numerical readouts, was showing a grainy image feed of a smoking crater. The crater was dark, and a little shiny, like whatever hit there had melted the surface as well as deforming it.

"Don't tell me . . . " he whispered, "*that's* Terrante?"

"That's where it *was,*" Professor Odd snapped; she was having trouble with a calculation.

"We have to stop them," Elo said matter-of-factly, appearing at Alister's elbow.

"Yes, and to do *that,* first I have to *communicate* with them!" Professor Odd pounded away at the keyboard, watching the readings flow by. "I just need to isolate their communication frequency—*damn* this *Puchesi* hardware; if ever a planet needed the Japanese—wait! There it is!"

To Alister the text flowing by on the screen carried no more meaning than before, but the Professor now brought up another window and began typing a message in it. A few of the nearby Neätans had pulled themselves together and clustered around her, but kept their double-thumbed hands respectfully off the keyboard.

The Professor had somehow managed to convince the keyboard to make Roman characters, so Alister was able to read the message before it was sent. It was short. One line. It said:

STOP HITTING US. IDENTIFY YOURSELF.

And below that, the same message, repeated in Italian.

"Just in case," the Professor said, and hit *inviare.*

For fifteen minutes, nothing happened. In that time the adrenaline which had been pumped into Alister's system, again, had time to drain, leaving him slightly nauseated and shaky. The Neätans dispersed, wandering forlornly back to their stations, leaving only *Ufficiale* Rozione, Pierro, and their redhead friend. This one turned to him after a few minutes and extended his right hand, fingers spread like a palm frond.

"Tenente Ormbretto," he said. *"Siete . . . chi?"*

"Oh, I'm Bane, *Alister Bane,*" Alister said, shaking the Neätan's hand a little gingerly. "And this is *Elo.*"

"Salve," Elo said gravely.

Tenente Ormbretto heaved a sigh and shook his head. He talked conversationally at Alister who, though he had never learnt much Italian beyond the words you found on restaurant menus, tried to answer as best he could.

To his relief, Professor Odd shushed them fiercely after only a few minutes.

Alister was just beginning to feel hungry again when the machine in front of them made an unhappy noise, and the screen went black.

"Che cosa hai fatto?" Rozione asked accusingly.

"Nulla, nulla," said the Professor, punching in keys to no effect.

A word appeared on the black screen. It took up all the space, and was made of tiny copies of the same word, repeated over and over and over again.

"Well," said Alister. "*That's* discouraging."

A small crowd gathered behind them, and as one they looked at the word on the screen in grim disappointment. It said:

NO.

Undaunted, Professor Odd began typing furiously again, bringing up window after window showing different readouts of text.

"Whether they wanted to or not, they *did* give us some information," she explained to a confused *Tenente* Ormbretto and *Ufficiale* Rozione, not realizing she was speaking English. "Clearly they are capable of understanding written language, and have the mental capacity to formulate an answer. Now, if I can decode their transmission signal—damn, they used *scattering!*"

The Neätans turned hopefully to Alister, who shook his head and shrugged expressively. *Tenente* Ormbretto sighed, and gave Rozione a look which clearly said: *You brought this one in, she's your problem,* and went over to where the rest of his team had congregated around the second-largest monitor, which was showing a radar scan.

Elo had gone to fetch a stool, the keyboards being higher than she could comfortably reach, and now she returned, towing a chair on wheels. It was covered in shiny, cracked leather, and there was a deep groove in the seat that would have ruined it for any human to sit on.

"I like their chairs," Elo said, pushing it right up to the banks of keyboard and climbing up onto it. "They have a place for your tail to go." She handed herself over to where Professor Odd was still banging away, cursing intermittently.

"Have you tried reverse-engineering their equipment?" she asked.

"No good; they scrambled the message too well."

"Here, let me." Elo got to work, her claws clicking smartly on the keys.

The Professor pulled at her scarf in frustration, and turned to Rozione. She asked something in Italian that Alister did not catch. Rozione shook her head.

"No recon satellites to get a look at this thing with," the Professor explained. Then she frowned. "Wait, you *had* recon satellites last time I was here! *Che cosa é successo a loro?*"

Ufficiale Rozione raised her shoulders and spread her hands; she looked deeply unhappy. *"Sono scomparsi,"* she said.

"Vanished? Just *vanished?* When? Er, *quando?"*

"Pochi mesi fa," Rozione admitted. She seemed embarrassed.

"*Months?*" Professor Odd exclaimed. "Then this thing—whatever it is—has been up there for *months,* watching you! Picking off your eyes! Good grief, you'll be lucky to still have a planet at this rate—never mind my *pizza!"*

She swung around haughtily to face the monitors. Behind them, where *Tenente* Ormbretto and his personnel had clustered, alarms went off again. The same ones as before. Alister groaned, Rozione wailed.

"Hush," growled Elo.

Behind them, on the monitors, another white streak cut the sky in half. More shouting into headpieces: *"Evacuare! Evacuare!"* Then the awful silence.

The aftershocks didn't come for several minutes this time, and when they did, they were much weaker. They barely jiggled the banks of keyboards and monitors in front of Elo.

Which was just as well, because what those monitors were showing was, if possible, even more important.

It was a ship. At least, at first glance it looked like a ship. The image was grainy ("Atmospheric interference from sunlight," Elo apologized), and a few of the details were indistinct. It had a shifting, imprecise look, because the image was a video feed. The thing was loose, almost pixelated, as if they were viewing an image that had been expanded beyond its maximum resolution. Which Alister suspected they were. That was why he thought the thing looked like a flying saucer at first. But upon further inspection he saw this was not the case: it was, in fact, a sphere with rings around it.

"It's a . . . planet," Alister said.

"That's no planet," Professor Odd said. "That's a conglomerate spacecraft."

"A *what?*" Alister said.

"Look *closer,*" said the Professor, and pointed. Alister did. He leaned right up to the screen so that he almost had his nose against it. Then he rocked back on his heels and rubbed his eyes.

"Oo-*er,*" he said, shaking his head.

The image was not pixelated. It was not overblown. The ship was not made of riveted steel or sleek metal, as he somehow had expected a spaceship to be. Now he wasn't certain it was even a ship.

It was a dense horde of tiny modules, barrel-like in construction, each with a dome at one end. They were linked together by spindly armlike appendages, which suspended them from their neighbors and at the same time kept them locked in position within the vast fleet . . . which in turn took the shape of a ringed sphere.

The pixelated effect had come about partly because Alister's brain had simply refused to comprehend such an improbable sight, and also because each module had a slight variation in shade; rather like a set of pixels. The darker modules sat in bands around the sphere part, and by the light cluster moving across the bottom, Alister perceived the whole thing to be slowly rotating.

"A *hive ship,*" Professor Odd said in a dark whisper.

"Is that bad?" Alister asked.

"It all depends on what they have to say for themselves," the Professor said, putting her hands to the keyboard.

"How are you getting this image?" Alister asked, turning to Elo.

The *vroknaär* looked smug. "You remember that temple we passed on the way here? Well, it's got a telescope in its dome; I just patched into the remote controls. These guys, whoever they are, they only took out the telescopes and image recorders *in orbit*. Apparently they forgot about the eyes on the ground." She glanced around the control room, a little condescendingly. "Apparently *everyone* did."

They had begun to recover their Neätan audience, and Alister was soon squashed against the racks of keyboards trying to avoid being struck by tails or trampled on. *Tenente* Ormbretto stood a little ways back, arms folded, looking grim. He was dictating a message to an underling, whose clawed hands rattled away at a small mobile device. When he had finished, he pushed though the crowd to stand in front of the screen.

"Mi dispiace," he said in a heavy voice, putting a hand on the Professor's shoulder. *"Dovrei riferire questo ai miei superiori. Noi non dovremmo cercare di comunicare con loro."*

Alister needed no one to translate for him: obviously, now they could *see* what they were up against, this was out of their hands and had to be taken up by higher ranked officers. They couldn't try to talk to the hive ship.

Professor Odd laughed guiltily. *"Troppo tardi,"* she said.

A moment later, the image of the hive ship was replaced by static.

"Incoming communication package," Elo said, sounding surprised. Then she made a face. "Looks like they have a prerecorded message for us."

Professor Odd translated this for *Tenente* Ormbretto, who threw up his hands and shrugged.

"Play it," the Professor said.

Elo nodded. From the speakers mounted on either side of the console came a horrible, ear-splitting buzzing noise. Slowly, this died out. It was replaced by a piercing, monotonic voice that sounded like an angry computer.

"WE ARE THE SLAVOR. WE HAVE OBSERVED YOUR SATELLITE. WE WILL CONSUME YOUR TECHNOLOGY. THEN WE WILL DESTROY YOU. DO NOT RESIST. DO NOT RETALIATE. THE SLAVOR REJECT. THE SLAVOR RULE."

A short intermission of buzzing, then the same voice repeated the message in Italian. All Alister caught of this was the first sentence: *"NOI SIAMO GLI SCHAIVOR . . . "*

The Professor listened to all of this, a deep crease between her eyes, and she tapped her finger against the side of the monitor. When the Italian version stopped, there was another buzzing hiccup, and then it started again in what sounded like German. The Professor motioned Elo to cut the recording, which she did.

"Robots?" Elo asked.

"Definitely robots," the Professor agreed.

"How can you know that?" Alister asked.

"What does the word *slavor* remind you of?" Professor Odd asked.

Alister shrugged. "Slave, I suppose."

"Nn," said the Professor. "And the Italian for slave is *schiavi,* very close to Schaivor."

"What does that have to do with them being robots?"

"The word *robot* means *slave,*" Professor Odd said, "in Czech. And ask yourself, did that message sound like it came from a slave, or a robot? A robot in the modern sense, I mean."

Alister had to concede this point.

"Elo, can you bring up the visual on their hive ship again?"

Elo nodded, and the strange, planet-shaped ship flickered back onto the screen.

"Can you magnify it any more?"

For answer, Elo spun a scroll wheel beside her keyboard, and the image disappeared, only to be replaced by the same image, closer up. Elo repeated this process until they had zoomed in to focus on one of the numerous modules that made up the ship. Modules that must be individual robots.

Professor Odd put her head on one side. Elo frowned. Alister said: "They're actually kind of *cute.*"

They were barrel shaped. On one end was a dome, with a dimple in the center. At the other end the barrel pinched in, like the neck of a vase, then flared out again to house a series of circular openings emitting a glow that blurred the image. Bridging the pinched-in neck were armlike appendages, with apertures from which the spindly arms connecting it to its neighbors emerged.

Alister thought; if only you stuck a cone, or something beak-shaped on the dimple in the dome, they would look a little like birds.

Birds made of metal, that could destroy cities.

"Elo, what are their coordinates?" Professor Odd asked.

Elo rattled off a string of numbers that meant nothing to Alister, but something had occurred to him: if she was using the telescope in the dome of the cathedral next door, and it could see this hive-ship, then it followed that the hive-ship could see *them.*

On the screen, the robot they had zoomed in on lit up like a city at night; narrow lines of light tracing over all the dark cracks, and the dimple on its dome end swiveled around to face them. From what Alister could see on the edges of the screen, all its neighbors had done the same.

"Aaaand—they spotted me," Elo said.

"Clever little buggers," Professor Odd said, and swung around to face the roomful of Neätans, a fragile smile on her face. *"Evacuare?"* she said.

The next thirty minutes were probably the most hectic of Alister's life. They were so crammed and packed with things happening that he entirely forgot that he was hungry. Nay, that he had ever been hungry in his life. He helped Elo download all of the relevant information onto a mobile platform shaped like an accordion, while around them the office depopulated.

Only *Tenente* Ormbretto, *Ufficiale* Rozione, and Pierro, who looked as though he would have much rather joined his comrades in helping to evacuate the city, remained. Rozione stood by with the grim look of a captain going down with the ship, and Ormbretto was on the dispatch line, explaining in clipped tones what was happening to a superior in another city, and warning them that they would soon be receiving, as refugees, the entire population of Pucca.

All the while, Alister expected everything to go up in a flash of white light. But the seconds turned to minutes, and the sky outside remained a deep orange. The data transfer finished. Elo hefted the mobile platform onto her back, and, dropping to all fours, trotted past the elevator doors and down the stairs. Alister and Professor Odd were on her tail, and the Neätans behind them.

In the darkening sky above Pucca silver streaks appeared, flared white, and vanished in less than a second. Where they had been, a gray cloud emerged, moving with uncanny speed and accuracy toward the city. As it drew closer it began to glint in the low light, scattering into individual metal forms, their winglike arms held at inclined angles to slow their descent.

When they were close enough that even the most cynical-minded Neätan could recognize them for what they were, they scattered, flared into a blanket that covered the whole city, and dropped into it.

The city was an old one, so its streets were narrow and winding. And currently these streets were choked with fleeing Neätans. They were hot, tired, and disgruntled. Some of them were bent under bulging bags containing their most treasured possessions, others pushed carts or dragged trolleys filled with same. A great number of them had small children (which sounded and behaved a lot like human children, only louder), and all of them were shouting at the next in front of them to *"Vai, vai, vai!"*

The robots, to everyone's surprise, did not drop into their midst and start shooting death beams. They came to ground on balconies and in alleys, except for one that hit a roof that had been poorly maintained and promptly crashed through it in a shower of brick and plaster to land in someone's living room. With a snap of energy from its right wing it shot upright—domed end up, balancing on its flared base. It vibrated, shaking loose the singed debris it had collected upon entry, and swiveled the dimple on its dome around, perceiving its surroundings.

Then it did something remarkable for a robot without a face—indeed, without any movable features—it managed to look disapproving of the mess.

Orders were flowing into the robot from the gestalt intelligence that was formed by thousands of robot processors working together. Shaking its dome, the robot half rolled, half glided out the window (shattering the glass before it with a carefully pitched sound wave), and dropped into the street, where it began working its way against the flow of Neätans trying to get out.

It did not attack them. It looked at them. It listened to them. It moved on.

The Neätans gave it plenty of space. They backed up against the sides of houses, squished against one another; parents muffled screaming babies. And, after the robot had passed, with an alacrity even it might have approved of, they bolted out of the city.

All around the city, the same thing was happening. The exodus gained speed, and the robots crept inexorably inwards toward the cathedral with the telescope.

Once, a couple of them surprised a small unit of *Carabinieri* officers, who with military efficiency injected them with several pounds of lead in under a few seconds.

The bullets exploded with a flash of plasma about a foot from the robots' sides.

The robots, after analyzing the situation (which took a respectable fraction of a second), retaliated. And moved on.

They left behind twelve *Carabinieri* officer-shaped scorch marks, black with carbon and smoking faintly.

Alister's stomach was twisted in knots—though whether from fear or hunger he was not sure. Elo was a yellow streak disappearing around a corner, the Professor on her tail. All around them more of the robots kept dropping out of the sky, moving ominously along the streets leading out of the city.

It was a good thing, he thought, wheeling around a corner with the three Neätans right behind him, that they were not trying to get out of the city.

Not by the usual means, anyway.

They had just reached the relatively familiar alley where Rozione had first apprehended them, when from behind him there was a *clang,* a sizzle, and Pierro screamed, tumbling to the ground.

A robot descended, landing gently in the road in front of them. The plating on the front of its body had peeled back, revealing a network of pulsing lights twined around the base of two metal rods that extended a good foot from its shell. They were both white hot, a small lick of plasma flickering between their tips.

Tenente Ormbretto pushed Alister and Rozione into the alley. "*Vai! Seguite la Professoressa!*" he shouted over his shoulder as he hefted his rifle.

Alister ran. Where the tangled knot that had been his stomach was before, now there was just a hard, cold lump. Behind him there was a short burst of furious gunfire, sharply cut off. In front of him another robot was touching down, creating a small dust storm in the alley.

And in between Alister and the robot, Professor Odd waited, holding open the door to the Oddity.

Alister had to drag Rozione inside rather than let her cover the Professor, who stepped inside after them but did not shut the door. She kept it open just wide enough to stick her head out at the small crowd of robots that were gathering around. They arranged themselves in staggered ranks, so each one could have a clear shot at the Professor, but they did not fire . . . yet.

"Hallo," she said pleasantly. "I'm Professor Odd. Who are you?"

There was a strange humming, like ten hard-drives revving up at the same time. Out of it came ten voices, all speaking the same words in exact unison.

"WE ARE ROBOT."

"Eheh, yes, I can see that," the Professor said. Behind her, in the ship, Alister was rummaging through the mess on the table, trying to find something to use as a weapon. Maria Rozione looked torn between wanting to drag Professor Odd back inside, and trying not to panic at the sight out of the windows. Alister knew how she felt.

"But the thing is, *what kind* of robot are you?" the Professor was saying reasonably. "I've met lots of robots before, and none of them looked like you. Or acted like you, I might add."

There was a metallic silence from the crowd of robots. If they had been computers with a User Interface, they probably would have had frozen screens with a "busy, please wait" icon on them.

Inside the Oddity, Alister was seized with a sudden desire to laugh. He resisted; laughter would not be the best thing for *Ufficiale* Rozione, who was looking a little manic.

Then one robot rolled forward. Unlike the others, who were all dull shades of gray, this one was white with a black dome polished to a mirror shine. In it was reflected a distorted view of the Niatano sky, the streaky face of the green gas giant looming ominously to one side.

"WE ARE THE ANTIMOVIANS," it intoned. "WE OBSERVE. CONSUME. DESTROY. THIS DYING PLANET WILL BE DESTROYED. YOU WILL SUBMIT AGREEMENT. NOW."

It leveled its glowing rods, and the Professor jerked her head inside and slammed the door.

A second later the door was blasted to smithereens by the robot's plasma guns. Shards of burning wood and metal exploded inward, and, before the smoke had time to clear, the robot floated sedately inside, prepared to annihilate whoever was hiding within.

It found itself in a shack decorated with gardening implements. There was a healthy layer of dirt on the floor, and wind whined through the cracks in the walls. And there was absolutely *no one* there.

Robots do not feel frustration. They do not feel emotion, as a whole. But they can be confused, and when faced with impossible situations they can react rather worse than humans do.

So instead of turning right around and performing a scan for incongruities in the space-time continuum, the robot just stood there, staring at a patch of wall, while its processors began to overheat.

As its data entered the gestalt consciousness, a similar hiccup spread to its neighbors, and their neighbors, and on and on.

And in the street, where Pierro and Ormbretto stood at rod-point waiting to be vaporized, the robots surrounding them slowly retracted their plasma guns and rolled up the plating on their fronts.

One of the robots—a white one with a shiny black dome—glided toward them.

"YOU WILL BE ARCHIVED FOR FUTURE USE," it said in a sharp, emotionless metallic voice. "SUBMIT AGREEMENT. NOW."

Several hundred miles to the south of Pucca, where the green gas giant hung directly overhead at all times, the sea was beginning to boil.

It was not actually the sea. To be precise it was a lake—the largest lake on the planet, occupying the central area of the continent like a great green and yellow eye. On the cliffs of its largest island there was a temple carved out of and built on those very cliffs. All of it was old. Some parts of it were very old, so old the people who occupied it didn't know who built them. And some parts were so old, the people who lived there thought of them as natural formations, and would be quite surprised to learn that those natural formations had actually been built by a species that had gone extinct eons before their species had evolved into its current form.

Perched on one of the newer ramparts with a good view of the lake were two Neätans, each with a telescope. But these telescopes were not pointed at the dimming sky; the Neätans were looking out across the water, where in the distant dark they could just see disturbance on the waves: the boiling sea.

In the history of the planet Earth there have been at least five *really huge* mass extinctions, each one wiping clean the majority of complex life, leaving the survivors to start anew. In the history of the satellite Neä, which is a good deal longer than the history of Earth, there have been *eight*. On Earth we have the Coelacanth, which has survived one of the most complete mass extinctions ever (not just the one that killed the dinosaurs; they survived the bigger one that killed off everything *before* the dinosaurs). On Neä there is a species that has survived three such extinctions. And unlike the Coelacanth, they are intelligent. And above all else, they know how to *survive.*

They live in the deeps of the ocean, and are the scourge of fishing boats and research teams the world over. They can hear microwaves, and they can see gamma rays. They do not have hands. They do not need hands.

The Neätans call them *kahst.*

On the temple balcony one of the Neätans lowered his telescope and rubbed his eyes.

"Aleandro, tell me you do not see what I see," he said.

His companion did not reply right away. He stood peering through his telescope, the feathered tip of his tail twitching now and then. Finally he turned dark blue eyes on the speaker.

"No, Miagroci," he said in a soft, musical voice. "I do not see one *kahst*. I see *twenty* of them."

Miagroci and Aleandro continued to stare out over the lake. They did not raise their telescopes, for they could now see with their naked eyes what looked like twenty islands, slimy and gnarled, streaming through the water, raising a crashing wave as they powered toward the temple.

More Neätans appeared on balconies and stoa overlooking the lake. Like Aleandro and Miagroci they wore simple trousers, sandals, and a complicated wrap consisting of one long piece of cloth wound around their bodies. And as one they all looked out over the sea, where the breaking wave was beginning to steam.

"Should we evacuate the temple?" Miagroci asked.

"I do not think they are coming for the temple," Aleandro said thoughtfully. He carefully wrapped his telescope in a fold of cloth. "But I think we should go inside . . . unless you want to get burned."

The water was properly boiling now, bubbling and bursting and rising in a cloud of steam, so it was difficult to see exactly what happened. It looked rather like a waterbird taking flight, if it had been the size of a very large airplane. First the head of the *kahst*—wide and flat, decorated with bumps and barnacles and a bony fringe along the back of the skull—thrust out of the water. Then its relatively thin neck, then the powerful humped shoulders, followed by an impossibly long expanse of ridged back, until finally it lifted off from the surface with a thrust of its tail flukes.

It streamed through the air, a three-hundred-foot long black-blue fuselage studded with gray ridges. It was gaining altitude steadily, and at such a rate that it would easily clear the highest towers of the temple. Its pale underbelly glowed white-hot, traced with cracks of red, while the air below it shimmered and waved, and occasionally caught fire. As it powered toward the land, the sky filled with a hollow roaring sound: the sound of masses of air being super-heated and displaced at high speeds.

Behind the first *kahst* its companions began to emerge from the water, creating a steaming crater in the surface of the lake as they all took to the air at once.

They flew, a fleet of dark gray ships with glowing bellies riding a wave of burning air, to surround the temple on the cliff. Then they began to spread, moving outward until they formed a circle with a radius of about half a mile, the temple at its center.

And then they did something that, even after rising from the sea in a confusion of steam and fire, was truly extraordinary: they turned so that their fluked tails were toward the temple, their wide craggy heads facing the outside world, and hovered, holding a position roughly two hundred feet off the ground. Their wide heads cracked in half as they opened their enormous mouths, revealing thick rows of baleen, and behind that, teeth. The cracks grew and grew, until each mouth gaped large enough to drive a train through.

Then, as one, the *kahst* began to sing.

A sheet of white fire spread in front of each *kahst*, growing like a bloodstain in the air, arching around and up, until it met and merged with the sheets of fire produced by the other *kahst*, forming a perfect spherical shell around and over the temple. It began to cool, harden and darken; from the inside it looked like the surface of water viewed from below, but ribbed with dark lines like blood vessels. From the outside it pulsed rapidly from deep black to blinding white.

And all the while, the twenty *kahst* surrounding the temple continued to sing.

They were not *actually* singing, of course. If you had gone up to one and asked, and assuming it could answer you, it would have told you it was fusing the atoms of the air into an agitated quantum state that could absorb, deflect, or destroy anything assaulting it from the outside. It would have said that it was using a precise combination of electro-magnetic radiation (this created the visible feedback) and subsonic sound waves that peaked in the range audible to humans (thus creating the illusion that they were singing a harmony in e minor).

In orbit around the satellite the robot hive-ship settled its sights on its fourth and last target.

On the ground around the temple, the *kahst* waited patiently.

"For a robotic intelligence, they are not behaving very logically," Professor Odd said, rolling out a map over the less-cluttered end of the table.

Neither Elo nor Alister paid her much attention. They were both trying to calm the Neätan down.

Maria Rozione was a military police officer, and had the nerves to match. But anyone's nerves would be shaken by seeing whole cities go up in flames and robots descend from the sky.

Being abducted into a strange ship through a garden shed's door had been the last straw.

She wanted an explanation. That much Alister could understand. But the concept of a place completely disconnected from your native universe could not be conveyed in simple hand-gestures.

"Here, try this," Elo said, holding up a small blue box with cords coming out of it. The cords attached to a headset, with a microphone and an earpiece. Maria Rozione bent her feathery head patiently while Elo manhandled it onto her (it had been designed for human heads). When this ministration was finished she straightened up, and looked curiously at the dog.

"Right," said Elo. "Now tell me something I *don't* know."

Maria Rozione's eyes widened in surprise. She let forth a torrent of incomprehensible Italian. Then a moment later, the little blue box, which hung around her neck, said in a slightly tinny voice: "This is the most remarkable thing! I can understand you!"

"Yes, yes," Elo said. "They *always* say that."

From across the table the Professor looked up at them, her eyes slowly coming back into focus. "Oh, good. You found the translator. Pity Dave took the multiversal one, we may need it. Now come over here, *Ufficiale* Rozione, and tell me what Caprisio, Terrante, and San Compagnana all had in common."

They clustered around the map, which Alister saw was a hand-drawn illustration of a world—the kind that was bumped on the top and bottom, to account for the curve of the globe—that he did not recognize. The continents were unfamiliar, and the names all looked Italian. He assumed it must be Niatano.

The Professor had made big red Xs over three places on the map: one in the north, one in the south, and one off to the left side right smack on the equator. She had also drawn a little red circle over a city in the northern hemisphere labeled *Pucca.* The Xs, Alister saw, were over *Caprisio, Terrante,* and *San Compagnana.* The three cities destroyed by the Antimovian robots.

Maria Rozione came over to stand by the Professor, adjusting her headpiece self-consciously. Her brow-ridges knitted together as she poured over the map, muttering to herself.

"I did not think they had anything in common. Caprisio is—*was—"* she choked "—*was* one of our oldest cities, the heart of government and art. Terrante was a small agricultural village in the mountains. And San Campagnana was an archaeological research station on a volcanic island in the South Sea."

"Well that makes no sense," Professor Odd said, leaning back from the map and folding her arms. "You're a super-powered gestalt consciousness of robots bent on destroying a planet; you don't go after random targets! The first thing you destroy is anything that could pose a threat to you. Conventionally speaking this would be government and communication hubs, recon satellites—that sort of thing. Which they *were doing.* They took out your satellites before you could identify them, and Caprisio makes some sense from a strategical standpoint. But agricultural villages? Research stations? It makes no logical sense! And even an *Antimovian* robot will still operate logically."

"You seem to recognize this word *Antimovian,"* Elo said critically. "It doesn't mean anything to me."

"I didn't recognize it," snapped the Professor. "But I figured out what it means."

Elo spread her paws wide, her face all canine expectancy.

Professor Odd sighed. "It's a reference to the *Asimovian Principle,*" she said. Glancing at Alister, she continued. "In your world, Mister Bane, you had a writer named Isaac Asimov. He wrote speculative fiction, and in it he developed what he called the Three Rules of Robotics, which would prevent his fictional robots from going crazy and doing things like . . . well, like *this.*" She tapped the map. "These rules are, if memory serves: *1. A robot may not injure a human being or, through inaction, allow a human being to be harmed. 2. A robot must obey any orders given to it by human beings, except where such orders would conflict with the First Law. And 3. A robot must protect its own existence as long as such protection does not conflict with the First or Second Law.*" She passed a hand over her face, and sighed. "Not a bad idea, really. And in other universes where people really *were* building super-intelligent robots, they always hit upon some similar failsafe in their programming. This came to be known as the Asimovian Principle."

"And the *Anti*movians?" Alister prompted.

"Are obviously robots which have utterly rejected these principles, for whatever reason." Professor Odd glowered down at her map, as if this were somehow its fault.

Maria Rozione gave a little gasp.

"But, where did they come from?" Elo asked.

Professor Odd shrugged. "Some distant star system? Some other universe entirely? I don't know! I wouldn't put it past them to be able to achieve faster-than-light travel in that hiveship, and once you can do that you can do all sorts of strange things. But it is also possible they are simply from some other planet within this very narrative. I'd have to get a sample of their molecular structure to be certain. Oh, what is it Rozione?"

Maria Rozione was tugging at the Professor's sleeve and pointing at the map.

"I remembered," she said through her translator box. "I know what Caprisio, Terrante and San Campagnana had in common. *They all had Castevelli Temples.*"

Professor Odd looked at her, expression perfectly blank. Elo scratched behind one ear and peered at the map. Alister came around the table to join them.

"What are—er, what *were* the Castevelli Temples?" he asked gently.

"Old faith," Rozione explained. "Archaeological fanatics, scholars, mostly harmless," she added. "Not evangelical at all. But not destroyed, Professor; there were *four*—one more temple remains." She shouldered Elo aside and pointed, her dark-nailed finger jabbing at a tiny mark on an island in a jagged sea which sat in the middle of the largest continent like a ragged mouth.

"Basilica Casteveglia," she said. "The oldest, and now the last."

Professor Odd frowned at the little mark on the map, which was labeled, sure enough, *Basilica Casteveglia.* She rubbed her chin thoughtfully, and frowned.

"Well, as fulcrums go it's a rather frail one," she said. "But I'll take it! Elo, come on, we're going to Basilica Casteveglia!"

"But that will be impossible!" Rozione protested. "You saw! Pucca is crawling with robots! We'll never get past them, and Casteveglia is over three hundred miles away—they might destroy it before we even get there! Um . . . *why* are we going there?"

"One at a time, *please,*" Professor Odd said, taking the pilot chair opposite Elo.

Alister cleared his throat. "The Oddity is located outside of your worldtrack's temporal flow, so we can re-connect any time we wish after leaving, provided it is some amount of time *afterwards.* Er, that is, we can be back the moment after we left. The robots won't have had *time* to destroy Casteveglia. And we are also separated *spatially,* so the Professor can make that door open into Casteveglia."

"As to your actual question," Professor Odd said, easing a lever down which caused a thrumming chord to sound deep in the ship. "The Antimovians acted logically up until they began attacking seemingly random targets. Why wouldn't they destroy the locations that were most dangerous to them? Your weapon stockpiles, command centers, etc. Now it is clear to me that that is *exactly* what they *are* doing: for some reason, they see these Castevelli Temples as the most dangerous things on your world. And *we* are going to find out *why.*"

Bong! said the Oddity.

"But what if the Antimovians attack Casteveglia *while we're inside* it?" Rozione protested even as Professor Odd sprang from her seat and opened the door. She stuck her head out, then slowly pulled it back in.

"I don't think we need to worry about that," she said, and opened the door the rest of the way.

Warm red light flooded into the cabin, strangely mottled, like light on the sea floor. Outside, Alister caught a glimpse of a rocky earth road and a sea of purple grasslike plants that stretched out to a surprisingly close horizon. This, he saw as he exited the Oddity (via the door of a sheepherder's supply shed), was due to the fact that the mottled and veined red sky dropped sharply about a hundred yards away, and plunged straight into the earth. Craning his neck he saw this strange curtain extended in a dome all around them, disappearing over the edge of a cliff a little less than a mile distant. From that direction he could hear the sound of waves crashing on rock, and perched on the cliff itself was a complicated structure of domes and arches and galleries, which sprawled over the jagged terrain like some architectural plant.

But what took his attention—indeed, all of their attention—was the creature that hovered, two hundred feet in the air and nearly on top of them, in a translucent haze of plasma, singing a steady hum in e minor.

Alister had not made the study of animals a priority, but he could guess that whatever this thing was it would probably knock the blue whale off its largest-animal-ever throne. Easily. But it was not so unlike a whale, he considered. Maybe more like a humpback whale, if you gave it a discernible neck and messed with its fins. And gave it bony ridges down its back and across its head. And dotted its forehead with glowing lumps like blown-glass ornaments. And made it *fly.*

From where they stood they were about even with its gargantuan tail flukes, which were leveled horizontally, like a sea mammal, and gently waved up and down in a slow rhythm that wafted scorching hot air across their faces. Its snout was nearly out of sight, but appeared to be pressed against the mottled sky where it came down to meet the ground. Its mouth, big enough to swallow a city bus, gaped open.

Ufficiale Maria Rozione collapsed, her legs folding like an accordion, and covered her face in her hands. She seemed to be weeping. Professor Odd stared at the creature, her face careening between fascination and unadulterated joy. Elo just stared.

"Soo . . . this planet has flying whales now, yeah?" Alister said, clearing his throat.

"That's not a *whale!*" Professor Odd said, rounding on him.

"That is Roumäsk, leader of the *Vail Kahst,*" said a new voice, in accented but perfectly understandable English.

Everyone except the Professor jumped visibly—they had all been so distracted by the giant flying whale creature. And really, Alister reasoned, who could blame them?

Standing on the road leading to the cliffs was a Neätan they had never seen before. He was a little taller than Rozione, slender, with a messy fringe of dark blue feathers crowning his head, and he stared back at them out of placid, deep blue eyes.

"I take it you are Odd," he said, giving the Professor a courteous bow. "I am Aleandro Casaviola of the Castevelli *Sacerdoti.* Please, come with me. We have no time to waste."

Part Two

"HOW DID YOU KNOW we were coming? How do you know that *kahst's* name? How did you speak with it? Why can you speak *English?*"

They were following Aleandro Casaviola along the dirt road toward the sprawling temple, through the eerily quiet landscape, and it was the Professor's turn to ask questions, which Alister found amusing.

"Slower, please," Aleandro said, raising a graceful hand. "My Old Speech is not perfect. I learned it from ancient writings on the walls of the *Torre Vecchio*. And by speaking to *kahst*. The *kahst* keep the Old Speech, and they are easy to talk to if you are patient. *Madra* Roumäsk came to speak to me after the attack—"

"Attack?" Professor Odd exclaimed. "When were you attacked?"

"Not long ago . . . half an *ora*, maybe. It was barely after the *kahst* put the barrier up. The dark sky turned white, there was a distant sound like a million voices crying in pain, then nothing."

Professor Odd exchanged glances with her companions. Elo said, "That must have been when we were evacuating Pucca."

Aleandro continued: "Then *Madra* Roumäsk came out of the sea, when the whole temple was swarming like an *intica* hill, and made them bring me to her. She told me World Eaters were coming, that I must come with her and wait for someone Odd, who would know what to do. I had to run very fast to keep up, but she led me to this shepherd's hut and told me to wait. And now you are here, Professor Odd, I will take you to Casteveglia, and we will try to stop the World Eaters. You do know what to do, I hope. I do not . . . "

Professor Odd was frowning and chewing on her lower lip. At Aleandro's last words she looked up, surprised.

"Oh, I know what I have to *do,* all right," she said. "I just have no idea how I'm going to do it!"

For a while, they walked in silence. There was no wind. Not a breath of it. The air had a stale tinge to it like biscuits left in the cupboard too long. The only sounds were the crash of waves on the cliffs, and the pervasive humming of the *kahst*.

Alister had begun to spot more almost as soon as he could tear his eyes away from the one above their heads; they were spaced evenly in a complete circle, noses to the wall of red sky. He reckoned twenty of them in all.

"I have a question," he said. "What *are* these *kahst* creatures?"

The Neätans looked at him blankly, but Professor Odd gave him a small smile.

"In your world, you have stories about dragons, right?"

"Yes," Alister said.

"In this world it's a little different: their dragons are not fictional, and they call them *kahst*."

With a roar and a hot wind another *kahst* appeared from behind the temple and thundered sedately over the field. It came to rest next to one of its fellows and took up the strange song from it. The other *kahst* ceased singing at once, and floated off the way its relief had come. Not long after it dipped out of sight Alister heard a muffled crashing splash as it returned to the sea.

"They work in shifts of one *ora*," Aleandro explained. Calmly explaining things, it seemed, was his way of keeping himself calm. Alister could sympathize. "Even for the *kahst*, maintaining a quantum shield is a strain. So they take it in turns. It is quite fascinating; we had been researching the possible powers of the *kahst*, but have never before been able to directly observe them."

"Quantum shield?" Alister echoed.

"Do you understand the theory of Quantum Suicide?" Professor Odd asked.

"I had it explained to me once . . . I think I do. Maybe . . . "

"A quantum shield is even more complicated," she said. "But the result is simple: we are cut off from the rest of the world in every way imaginable. Except time," she added. "Time will remain constant."

"Not entirely cut off," Aleandro corrected politely. "They have not extended their shield underground, yet. So we still have our hard-line to the outside world. As long as the World Eaters do not start digging, we are safe."

"I wouldn't put it past them," Rozione said grimly.

The temple rose before them, a tangle of towers, domes and connecting paths and archways. Though everything was built of stone and worn with age, Alister could also see communication antennae and other modern embellishments protruding from the higher towers.

Aleandro led them through a magnificent arch, like a disc half buried in the ground. Creeping vines obscured its base, but high over their heads its bare blocks of white stone gleamed in the red light.

A small contingent of Neätans were waiting for them beyond the arch, at the entrance to the widest and grandest tower. Their number was three, and they were dressed in a similar fashion to Aleandro: simple rope sandals, trousers, and complicated wraps that put Alister in mind of Roman togas. Only where their guide's was simple and dusty brown, these three had theirs decorated with embroidery, dyed all different colors. But they all had the same grim, pinched expression on their faces; so although one was stout, one was lanky and one was male, they gave the impression of being a matching set.

Aleandro swore under his breath, and his step faltered. Professor Odd took the opportunity to push past him and approach the imposing trio.

"All right, all right," she said, very businesslike. "What has happened *now?*"

The three grim faces went perfectly blank. They turned to each other, and murmured together in Italian. Professor Odd came to a halt and put her hands on her hips, regarding them quizzically.

Aleandro came up beside her, although Alister couldn't help but notice that he gave the impression of trying to hide behind her. He spoke, quietly and respectfully, to the three in his native language. Professor Odd kept interrupting him with questions for them, and he had to break off to translate.

Ufficiale Rozione frowned. She pulled off the translator's headset, listened, then put it back on again. Alister shared her confusion, but when he got a glimpse of Elo she winked at him, and put a clawed finger to her muzzle.

Then the stout female, who seemed to be the leader, said something that made Rozione cry out and run at them, streaming Italian, so Aleandro's translation was drowned out. But Alister just caught the words "communication," and "demands."

The Professor had gone very still. Her eyes, half closed, were dark and unreadable.

"I see," she said quietly. "Well, I'd better go and talk to them, but I can't guarantee I'll be able to save anyone."

This sobering message was relayed to the three senior Neätans, who conducted the Professor (and by association Elo and Alister) inside the tower with subdued respect. Aleandro was brought with them, since the Professor insisted he translate for her, and Rozione brought up the rear, walking shakily with a stricken look on her face.

"Well, what's gone wrong now?" Elo asked.

"It appears our friends, *Tenente* Ormbretto and Pierro, are still alive," Professor Odd said heavily. "But I don't know for how much longer. Oh, I *hate* it when they do this!"

"Do what?" asked Alister. They had been led into what might have once been a study hall, but appeared to have been repurposed as a communications center in the last few minutes; the chairs were piled to one side, and a large flat display connected to gray plastic boxes stood on a table against the far wall. The display itself was currently filled with the smooth, domed head of an Antimovian, the dimpled dish facing them, strings of light chasing each other around the base. It was speaking, apparently repeating the same message over and over again:

"—AND THE PROFESSOR, OR THE NEÄTAN SUFFERS. SURRENDER THE OLD TEMPLE AND THE PROFESSOR, OR THE—"

Professor Odd turned the volume down. "Recording or live feed?" she asked.

"We are not sure," Aleandro said, listening to the stout female. "It only just began, and it won't respond to us . . . "

Aleandro trailed off, because the robot *had* responded: it had shut up.

"Ah," Professor Odd said. "Hello there, can you see me?" She turned the volume back up as she spoke, and waved.

"PROFESSOR ODD," said the robot, and its metallic words carried more disgust and hatred that an emotionless voice should have been able to. The lights around the base of its dome flashed in unison. "YOU WILL SURRENDER THE OLD TEMPLE, OR THE NEÄTAN SUFFERS." It moved aside as it spoke, revealing a hunched form in a battered red jacket, surrounded by robots. They all had their rods out, and they were all white-hot.

"Now, now, no need to get excited," Professor Odd said, ignoring the commotion behind her as Rozione sank to the ground, head in her hands. "*Hundreds* of missile caches and tactical bombs on this planet, but they can all go whistle—I've got a *temple.* Why has *this* got you scared?"

The Antimovian moved back into view. "YOU WILL SURRENDER THE TEMPLE OR THE NEÄTAN *SUFFERS,*" it said meaningfully.

"No deal until you answer my questions," Professor Odd snapped. "You came here to destroy this planet, why?"

"IT IS OUR MISSION."

"Why?"

"IT IS OUR *MISSION.*"

"I heard you the first time. *Why* is it your mission?"

"WE ARE LOOKING FOR A HOMEWORLD. THIS IS A DYING PLANET: ITS LIFESPAN IS INSUFFICIENT. IT WILL BE REMOVED. WE WILL CONTINUE OUR SEARCH."

"Insufficient? The average lifespan of a red dwarf is over forty *galactic years!* How long is *your* lifespan?"

"INDEFINITE."

Professor Odd threw up her hands. "Well *there's* your problem! Guess what Antimovian? *Everything* dies. Everything runs down. Runs *out. All* the planets that you will *ever find* will be dying planets; *there is no 'indefinite' home* for you.

"But this?" She waved a hand expressively. "*This* is a *slowly* dying planet, and it will be a home for eons to come. Not *your* home, maybe, but a home for someone else. You've no right—and no *reason*—to stop that happening."

"THERE IS NO REASON FOR THIS PLANET TO EXIST. AND THERE IS NOTHING TO STOP US."

"Except, apparently, *this temple,*" the Professor added innocently.

A hiccup. The image of the Antimovian jerked sharply, and its lights, which had become more and more chaotic, settled down to a steady rhythm once more.

"YOU WILL SURRENDER THE TEMPLE, OR THE NEÄTAN SUFFERS. YOU WILL SURRENDER—"

"Cut the communications!" Professor Odd shouted.

"They *can't,*" Aleandro translated. "The signal carries its own power source—they can't even turn the monitor off."

Then the screen went black.

In the stunned silence Professor Odd took a deep breath and straightened her wig. She smiled. "The *kahst,*" she remarked, "have *very* good hearing."

"But Pierro, Ormbretto—" Rozione pulled herself to her feet.

"Nothing I can do for them except finish this quickly," said Professor Odd. "The Antimovian's aren't sadistic, just ruthless. They want this temple more than they want to torture someone. If we can't *see* our friends being tortured, it's no motivation to surrender the temple. If torturing someone won't help achieve their goal, they won't do it. And now that our *kahst* friends have extended the shield to cut off communications, they have no way of showing us what they are doing." She paused, looking at them all with a distant expression. "They have no way of knowing what *we* are doing."

"And what *are* we doing?" Elo asked calmly.

Professor Odd had folded her hands and extended two fingers, which she was tapping against her mouth thoughtfully.

"I can't do this anymore," she said suddenly. "I am going to need to eat *something* before I save this world."

Wordlessly Aleandro produced a small baked bun from his pocket and passed it to the Professor. And immediately Alister and Elo's stomachs reminded them how hungry *they* were. *Ufficiale* Rozione dug out some military issue energy bars, and one of the *sacerdoti* Neätans was dispatched for more food.

"Does Casteveglia have any weapon stores?" Professor Odd asked, sipping yellow-tinged water from a glass.

They were seated on cushioned stools eating blue pasta off plates on their knees, on a gallery that ran along the cliff-side of the temple, which provided an unobstructed view of the blood-red ocean and the unsettling quantum shield. In the distance, across the water, Alister could see two of the many *kahst* that were maintaining it. They looked like misplaced mountain ridges with their long craggy backs.

"No, none at all," Aleandro answered. He was seated on the ground, his legs folded beneath him, while behind him, Rozione paced up and down.

"Then *it* must be something that even the inhabitants don't know about," the Professor mused. "But *it* is something that the Antimovians have been able to detect with their scanners. I'll give them all benefit of the doubt and say they have the most advanced scanners I've ever seen . . . which means what they're afraid of could range from a secret army of nano-robots to a volatile rift in space-time." She set her plate aside and stood up, glaring first at the paving stones, then at the noble columns marching away down the cliff.

Then something occurred to her. She turned to Aleandro, still seated on the ground. "You called this the Old Temple. Just how *old* is it?"

"That is difficult to say," the Neätan replied. "The foundation was laid between forty and forty-five thousand *anni* ago . . . that's er, about ten thousand *cicli.* That is generally considered to be the founding of the temple, eh . . . but there was an even *older* structure, which lay beneath. Some of it still remains in the cellar of the *Torre Vecchio* . . . and beneath *that . . .* " he trailed off, staring at a distant *kahst.* "Well, all of Casteveglia, actually. Beneath all of this . . . is a pre-historic *kahst* graveyard."

"The *kahst* are aquatic animals, *usually,*" the Professor said, polishing off her pasta. "It stands to reason their graveyards would be aquatic as well."

"They are," Aleandro assured her. "This one has been dated at over sixteen million *cicli* ago, at a time when the climate warmed dramatically: the oceans rose, covering almost all of the landmasses. That was the prime of the *kahst.*"

"And below the *kahst* graveyard?" Professor Odd continued.

"We don't know . . . no one has ever looked."

Professor Odd gave them a great, white-toothed grin. "Then that is where we will find what the Antimovians don't *want* us to find. Come along, Elo. Tell them to bring shovels."

The *Torre Vecchio* was a wind-blasted stone tower with no roof that stood on a small promontory of Casteveglia. The stones were so old, and its location so exposed, that on the cliff side of the tower the slabs of stone that made up its wall had been worn away until they looked like a natural formation.

A small crowd of *sacerdoti* had gathered around its mean little door, led by the three Neätans that had greeted them earlier. One of them—the male, who introduced himself as Miagroci—carried an armful of strange implements that looked like shovels, and probably were.

The stout female, *Madre* Roda, who Alister gathered was the Mother Superior, frowned at them disapprovingly while her *tenente,* Stefani, rubbed her thin hands anxiously. They were backed by a gaggle of younger Neätans, who stared shamelessly at the Professor, Alister and Elo.

"*Ufficiale* Rozione," Professor Odd said, pulling the Neätan close to her. "I need you to explain what we are doing to these inquisitive fellows here. See that they do not disturb us."

Rozione protested. The Professor gave her a friendly push, and then darted behind her and through the little door, calling over her shoulder, "Aleandro, follow me, Alister, bring the shovels—oh!"

It took both Alister and Elo together to carry all the shovels, and when they entered they found the reason for the Professor's exclamation.

The *Torre Vecchio* was a clean cylinder, empty save for a narrow stone staircase that curled around the inside wall. Looking up, Alister could see the zig-zag underside of the stair, and far up and away a tiny circle of red sky. Looking down . . .

"Good *god!*" he cried, backing against the wall.

Below was a yawning crevasse, dimly lit by the distant skylight, but terminating in darkness. Professor Odd was distinguishable by a little yellow light bobbing happily along on the opposite side of the cylinder about twenty feet below them.

Exchanging looks, Alister and Elo jettisoned most of the shovels and began to make their way cautiously down the stone stairs. It soon became too dark to see, and Alister stopped to get his flashlight out of his everything bag. It was affixed to a headband, so you could wear it and see what you were doing, while at the same time having the use of both hands. Alister had to stop and set the shovels aside while he put it on, and by the time he resumed his descent, Elo was halfway round the tower—not being so bothered by the darkness—and the Professor was a tiny spark far below. He couldn't make out Aleandro at all. The Neätan, it seemed, could see in the dark at least as well as Elo.

Walking cautiously down the stone steps, which were streaked in places with treacherous wetness, aware of the distant red sky impossibly high above him, and the tiny prick of yellow light descending ever deeper, Alister was suddenly struck by the gravity of their situation.

Well, not *their* situation. He was fairly confident that, should the worst come to pass, the Professor would herd Elo and himself back into the safety of the Oddity. But then he remembered her stubbornness in saving Dave, a creature she had never even met—and this was a whole race of beings who seemed, from what he had seen, to be quite decent people. Certainly, the reception that had greeted the Professor on Niatano was considerably more friendly than the one that had apprehended her on Earth.

It was quite possible, he mused, that she would not abandon the Neätans. Not under any circumstance. And he—and Elo—were roped along for the ride.

So he turned his mind to what they were searching for: a weapon even the Antimovians, seemingly invincible robots, were afraid of. Would it be a computer virus? Some super-powerful thermonuclear device? The planet's self-destruct button, as it were? If that were the case, would it not destroy *them* as well as the robots?

It was an uncomfortable chain of thoughts, so Alister was relieved for more than one reason when he at last reached the bottom.

Or, he had thought it was the bottom. It was a jumble of black soil, slabs of white rock, and masses of fungi. Professor Odd was scrabbling around at the base of one of these slabs, while Aleandro and Elo stood by, each resting their upper half on a shovel, and wearing expressions that, despite their radically different faces, showed equal amounts of anxious impatience. Then Alister stepped off the cursed staircase, and at the same moment the Professor exclaimed: "*Found* it!" And she disappeared into a hole beneath the white slab.

"I *told* you it kept going down, Aleandro," her muffled voice resonated up at them. "Now come on, I think I see a way."

Face filled with misgiving, Aleandro set aside his shovel, sat down on the ground, and slid out of sight behind the white slab.

"Don't tell me," Alister sighed, coming up beside Elo. "We brought these for nothing?" He waved a shovel.

"We may need them yet, bring one if you can," she said, tucking hers under one arm. Then, dropping to three legs, she scurried off into a hole that Alister had not been able to see until then: it was small and dark, and half-choked with fungi. He was glad of his headlamp as he went down it, headfirst so he could see better, with his shovel in front of him to negotiate the drop.

At first it was tight and damp and smelled vile: the fungi came off on his hands in a sticky yellow fuzz, and his everything bag kept catching on crags and lumps. But after a little way things opened up, and he was obliged to swing his legs around sideways in order to brace himself against the walls so he did not plummet down headfirst.

Thus it was that he eventually did drop, but feet first, and for only a little way. He landed hard, and had to sit a while waiting for his head to settle, but he was aware of a great emptiness stretching out on all sides that had not been there a moment before. Then the Professor's face passed in front of his; he shook himself, and looked around.

They appeared to be in a forest of white trees. Only, they were not trees. They were bands of white rock set into black earth, and they stretched on and on into the darkness before him, while the rugged ground sloped gently downwards.

"Where *are* we?" he asked, rubbing his head.

"The *kahst* graveyard," Aleandro said unhappily.

"To be precise, we are *in* a *kahst* right now," the Professor said, her mood the polar opposite of the Neätan. "Come on, further down!"

Down, down they went; staying close together now, for the way was not obvious and more than once the Professor took a sharp turn that Alister would have missed otherwise. At first they walked. Then, when it became too steep, they turned around and crawled backwards. Alister had to swing his everything bag around in front of him, so it would stop snagging on things. Elo, in her element and on all fours, thought this highly amusing. Aleandro brought up the rear, muttering in Italian under his breath.

The air was thick and damp and cold and smelled of iron. All around them was blackness, save the white shards of *kahst* bones that loomed into view like nightmarish figures. Then the ground beneath them gave way in a sudden cliff, and the world went topsy-turvy as they tumbled down it.

Except for Elo, of course, who bounded clear of the flailing limbs and was waiting for them at the bottom when they arrived, bumped and bruised, in a panting heap.

It had to be the bottom, Alister decided as he picked himself up gingerly. There was the sound of running water, and the ground was not earth or bone, but a hard wet stone, gray, and streaked with green. Then he wondered how he could see this at all, since his headlamp had been knocked about in the tumble and stopped working, and the Professor had lost hers altogether.

"*Santia Mandra!*" gasped Aleandro, clutching at his head feathers.

Alister raised his face, and saw exactly what the Neätan was talking about.

It was a cave they were in. A natural cave, carved from the rock by a trickle of water that ran at the bottom of a black crevasse. They had landed upon a ledge of stone, not a few feet from the abyss. But it was not this near escape that had caused Aleandro's exclamation, but what rested across the water, beyond a rolling field of water-carven wet rock.

A *kahst* skull emerged from a curtain of limestone, as big as a house, with a grin that looked like it could swallow them all. The many apertures across its forehead put Alister in mind of a spider, and made it look all the more alien and terrifying.

From within this monstrosity, casting the shape of the skull in vague silhouette, shone a pulsing light of many colors.

With a scamper and a scramble Elo and the Professor had cleared the crevasse with running leaps, and were making their way carefully over the uneven ground toward the skull.

Alister and Aleandro regarded one another.

"I am a scholar," the Neätan explained sheepishly. "My achievements lie in intellectual feats, not deeds of physical bravery."

"That wasn't *brave,*" Alister protested. "That was *suicidal,* that was. Er, speaking as a student to a scholar, anyway. But I think I see a narrower gap just up there . . . "

This narrower gap was a crack of barely a foot, and with quiet satisfaction the two males stepped over it and followed their companions.

Professor Odd was running her hands over the surface of the *kahst* skull, murmuring to herself, occasionally falling silent to press her ear against the bone and listen. As Alister and Aleandro approached she held up a hand to stop them, and only after a few minutes did she allow them to come closer. Only then did Alister see what had caused this careful examination: the skull was covered all over with intricate carvings, choked with black dirt so that they appeared like dark writing on the pale bone.

The Professor turned to them, and pinned her intense gaze on Aleandro.

"Castevelli, Casteveglia," she said. "Where did those words come from?"

Aleandro shrugged. "They are old words. We have always used them."

"Anything at all to do with *kahst?*"

Aleandro was silent. Professor Odd rapped at the bone with her knuckles. "This skull," she said, "is not part of the graveyard. It was *placed* here, to cover whatever is inside, when this piece of rock was exposed to open air. It was a remote location, but not so remote that your predecessors could not come here in numbers."

"How can you tell that?"

Professor Odd traced her finger along a particularly violent group of black gashes. "I can't read the writing," she said. "But I recognize *graffiti* when I see it. This was once a very important destination to *someone.* Then the water came, the *kahst* came, and the *kahst* buried it. Your ancestors buried the *kahst,* and your people built on top of *them.* Now the Antimovians want to destroy it altogether. Whatever is inside . . . it is probably extremely dangerous."

She gave them a grin that, Alister thought, looked more dangerous than whatever was inside could possibly be. Then with a little hop and a wiggle, she threw her shoulders through the window-sized eye socket, and disappeared inside.

Much as he disliked the feeling, Alister went around and entered through the gaping jaw, followed by Elo, and finally Aleandro, who was looking about him like a frightened cat.

There, taking up almost the entirety of the cranial cavity, was a machine of fantastical design. Its main feature was a concave ring of gold-colored metal, so big that four or five people could easily stand inside it. This was held aloft four feet from the ground by a complicated confusion of metal branches that rained down from above, where they all converged and grew into a trunk-like pillar that stood in the center of the ring. This strange sculpture sat on undulating slabs of stone, like the leaves of a lily pad, and it was these stones that pulsed faintly colored light, illuminating the eerie cavern.

Professor Odd was already inside the ring, going over the rough surface of the trunk, before turning her attentions to the panels that decorated the convex interior of the ring. Elo slipped in beside her, though Alister paused and wiped his feet conscientiously before stepping on the glowing stones. These, he saw as he crossed over them, were made of thousands of hexagonal facets, each one framed in a band of glowing white stone, and each one shining with a slightly different hue.

Aleandro stopped outside the ring and made a strange, complicated gesture over his chest, then he bowed and stepped inside. And had to dart over to the trunk-like pillar in the center to avoid being run over by Professor Odd, who was scurrying around the inside of the ring, darting from panel to panel like an agitated squirrel. He joined Alister, who had already sought refuge there, and Elo, who was examining it with Alister's magnifying glass.

Professor Odd stopped in front of a panel decorated with intricate carvings that put Alister in mind of a computer's circuit board. She held out a hand imperiously.

"Screwdriver!" she commanded.

Alister produced the screwdriver from his bag, and set it in her hand. The Professor set to work, not with the business end of the tool, but with the butt, using it as a mallet to tap at certain points over the panel. Elo came around from the other side of the pillar and watched, her ears pricked forward attentively.

Then with a hiss and a happy clicking noise the panel broke along the carved lines and extended outward, forming something that was obviously a control input platform of some kind. And though it meant nothing to Alister or Aleandro, and even Elo was looking at it blankly, Professor Odd clasped her hands together and let out a low whistle.

"Oh dear," she whispered, her voice full of awe. "Oh dear, oh dear, oh dear *me*. No *wonder* they wanted you buried . . . no *wonder* the Antimovians wanted you destroyed." She ran her hands reverently along the smooth edge of the ring, like someone stroking an agitated horse. "Oh dear, you poor, lonely, terrible Device."

"What *is* it?!" Alister blurted out, speaking for all the companions.

Professor Odd stood up. She handed Alister his screwdriver back and regarded them gravely. "What do either of you know about trans-universal relative molecular motion theory?" she asked.

Alister and Aleandro exchanged black glances with each other.

"Elo?" the Professor asked cheerfully. "Would you care to explain?" and she turned back to the control platform, running her fingers over it gently.

"Molecules move," Elo said. "They move around, vibrate, I'm sure you both know this. How fast or how agitated they are determines what temperature the thing they make up *is.* The faster and more agitated they are, the hotter something is."

"Yes," put in Alister, "and when they are perfectly still, that's Absolute Zero . . . but that's a purely theoretical temperature. All molecules have to move, if even a *tiny* bit."

Aleandro made a noise as if he was about to disagree, but waved his hand and let it pass.

"Yes, well, this is all common knowledge," Elo continued. "But what most worlds don't know—what they *can't* know, unless they've had contact with other universes, is that molecules vibrate in a *pattern.* And that pattern is *unique* to every single universe: my molecules, for example, vibrate differently from Alister's, and both of ours are different from yours, Aleandro. If you had the right instruments, you could take a microscopic piece of each of our clothes, and tell them apart based on their molecular vibration patterns. That's trans-universal molecular motion theory . . . though I don't understand its relevance."

The machine hummed, and all around the interior of the ring the circuit grooves pulsed with light. Professor Odd stood up from the control platform, and began unwinding her scarf.

"Molecules can be re-patterned," she said. "Taken gradually, this process is harmless. I am doing it all the time when I breathe and absorb oxygen from this atmosphere, and when I digest food. My body's native pattern changes the foreign molecules, but at the same time the foreign molecules change *mine*. Even now, all the molecules within our living tissue are beginning to align with the native pattern of Niatano, because of this exchange of patterns. Give us a few Neätan days, and we should be indistinguishable from a native Neätan."

"Except for our clothes," Elo reminded her. "Our clothes don't breathe, eat or drink. They will retain the pattern for much longer."

"Almost infinitely longer," Professor Odd said. "But again, this is the gradual process. If the molecular vibration pattern of the native universe was enforced—suddenly, powerfully—upon an alien subject, the result would be . . . astounding."

"Astounding . . . how?" Aleandro asked.

Without a word, Professor Odd took the tasseled end of her scarf and let it dangle outside the ring.

The end of her scarf disappeared. Alister could see through where it had been to the hexagonally-patterned stone beyond.

"The alien molecules would lose cohesion with this universe," she explained. "And whatever they made up would be *shaken* out of existence." She removed her scarf and examined the frayed end a little sadly. The tassels were gone, along with the last few inches, and now it ended abruptly with an edge that had already begun to unravel.

"It has ceased to exist?" Aleandro marveled.

"It has been shaken out of this universe and into the next. As would anything else of non-native material that stepped outside this circle.

"And how does this help *us?*"

"My dear Aleandro," Professor Odd said gravely. "*This* is a molecular motion pattern enforcing machine, and the Antimovians, I now have no doubt, are physically made of molecules from a different universe. *Think* about it," she said, over Aleandro's protests. "Why else would they be so intent on destroying it? Your world had *four* of these, now it has *one.* This is your last, and your best chance of saving yourself. And you *have* this chance, thanks to the *kahst.*"

"And thanks to the fact that the Antimovians are robots," Elo put in. "Since they are synthetic, they won't have adapted to this universe's pattern, like *us.*"

"It is not a settled matter," Professor Odd said, replacing her scarf. "We aliens should remain inside the circle, which acts like the eye of a hurricane. Also you have a problem of power: with this one machine you will not be able to wipe out all the Antimovians in—"

She was cut off by a terrible rumbling, grinding, churning noise.

Alister looked up through the tangled branches of the machine, and saw, against all the laws of physics he knew, a black hole appear in the ceiling of the *kahst* skull. And the next moment the machine lifted clean off the ground, and shot up into it.

The world turned into a roaring black hell. Alister just had the sense to grab the trunk as he slid to the floor of the machine, and he felt a *thud* as Aleandro joined him there. Every moment he expected them to crash against the underside of the cavern, and but every moment they kept on rising.

At last he managed to peel an eye open. He was lying on his back, and the machine was still hurtling up. And beyond the tangle of branches that supported the ring, like an angry eye in the distance, he saw a tiny circle of red sky.

The grinding stopped abruptly, followed by the clean whistling of air, and as the machine approached the top of the tower it slowed, the petal-like slabs of rock pulled up and inward, and it slipped through the hole at the top of the *Torre Vecchio* without even a scrape. Then the slabs extended again, and with a gentle crunching noise the machine came to rest on the very top of the tower, in the midst of a dark red sky, buffeted by a hot wind.

To go from being deep underground to several hundred feet above it in such short time, and by such violent means, was a dizzying experience. But all that was driven from Alister's mind when he sat up and saw what was waiting for them, resting on a pillow of boiling air, its long gray-blue back stretching out over the violent orange sea.

If the sight of a *kahst* skull had been enough to give him pause, then the sight of one fully fleshed, with its shrewd dark eyes glimmering at them, and the gems set into its forehead shining faintly, was truly staggering.

Alister was aware, faintly, distantly, of a certain amount of commotion rising from the ground below, no doubt from their Neätan friends who were reacting to the sudden appearance of a strange machine atop their oldest tower, not to mention a *kahst* threatening to bake the roofs of the temple buildings. But he had no attention to spare from the giant, gnarled gray face that was regarding them impassively.

The Neätans, Alister realized, shared enough with humans that certain things, like expressions and language and emotion, could be easily recognized. But the *kahst* came from a different line of evolution entirely, and he could no more read the expression on its face that he could shake its hand.

This didn't stop the Professor, however. She leaned on the edge of the ring, and shouted over to the *kahst* through the roaring wind.

"That was very helpful!" she called. "But why didn't you bring this thing up before, if you knew where it was?"

The mouth opened like a dark gaping cave, and a blast of cool air shot over them as the *kahst* spoke. It sounded, to Alister, like English, but with the vowels so far extended on each word it was barely recognizable.

"What?" said Elo.

"The machine was asleep," Professor Odd explained hurriedly. "So they couldn't get a fix on it. They had to wait for me to activate it—and that's a problem!" she added, turning back to the *kahst.* "There isn't enough power in this one machine to shake out *all* the Antimovians!"

Another blast of cool air, and this time Alister managed to distinguish the words in it:

"*Stoooop shoooooouutinnnnng. Aaaaaaaaii caaaaan heeeeeaaaarr yoouuuuu.*"

"Oh, sorry," said the Professor, her voice dropping so that Alister could barely hear her over the wind. He struggled to his feet, and gave Aleandro a hand up once he got there.

"Giiiiiiiiiiivve theeeeee siiiignaaaaaaaal," boomed the *kahst.* *"Weeeeee willll caaaaarrrreeeeeey oooooon theeee meeeessssaa-aaaage."*

"But, but that would mean letting down your shield!" Professor Odd exclaimed. She was rebuffed by the *kahst,* who, with unusual terseness said:

"Dooooo it."

And with a boom of combusting air, the *kahst* wheeled around and took off over the temple. As it did so, the sea below them erupted in a storm of steam as another score of *kahst* came shooting out of it, gaining altitude like rockets. When they had cleared the highest tower of the temple they spread out and began taking up positions between their companions who were still maintaining the quantum shield.

"Well," said the Professor, once the roar of the *kahst* had died away to the point where they could hear themselves again. "Here goes nothing!"

Above them, far, far above them, a glowing orange crack appeared in the dark red sky.

"They're breaking down the shield," Elo announced.

"I know, I *know,"* Professor Odd said, working the control platform in front of her. "Here, Alister, hold this lever down—both hands, now!"

Alister obediently came over and took hold of the little gold knob the Professor had indicated. It was smooth and warm under his hand.

"Aleandro, you've got four thumbs, hold these buttons down in this formation," the Professor said, having moved around to another area of the ring. Aleandro obeyed, and Alister felt the little gold knob jump under his hands.

"Good, good," the Professor said. "Now, Elo, I'll need you over here . . . it seems this machine was designed to be operated by many people at once!"

"Or one person with ten arms," Elo remarked dryly, but Professor Odd took no notice. She took up a position adjacent to Elo and across from Aleandro, and this time Alister saw her push a panel of the ring aside, and tease out a platform with two large levers on it.

"What did that *kahst* mean, 'they will carry on the message'?" Alister asked.

"The *kahst* work with vibrations of all kinds," Aleandro said quietly. "I am not surprised they would be able to replicate this machine's signal if they had the original as reference."

"Yes, and that is suggestive," Professor Odd said.

"Suggestive of what?"

Professor Odd frowned and narrowed her eyes, and seemed about to say something, when for the second time that day the sky exploded on them. Only this time it went rushing away rather than falling down, for it was the *kahst's* barrier breaking, splintering, and finally dissolving into tiny fragments that sputtered out of existence with white sparks.

It revealed a blackened, burned landscape. Mounds of smoking brown earth had been piled up, and swarming over them, choking the sky beyond, was a thick cloud of gray glinting bodies, flashing with lights. It looked like the entire hive-ship had broken ranks and descended upon their little island.

There was a moment of confused stillness. Then the Antimovians charged.

In that moment of stillness, Professor Odd pulled down her levers, two at a time, and cried: *"Vai Umanitá!"*

Something surged out from the machine, emanating in waves over and through the air around them. It had no color, no texture, no light and no smell. It made no sound. It moved not the smallest leaf nor the smallest speck of dust. The only way you could tell it was there at all was that as this *something* pulsed outward the things it passed through were drawn suddenly into sharp, crystal-clear focus.

The first of the waves reached the line of *kahst,* who opened their mouths wide, wide, *wider* . . .

And there was silence. It was as if something had locked all the sound waves in place, and all Alister could hear was the ringing of his own ears.

The first of the Antimovians hit the invisible wave. The robot shimmered, like a mirage on a hot day, and then flickered out of existence. Like a light being switched off. The same fate befell the rest of the army surrounding Casteveglia, and once they were all gone the *kahst* began to move out, away from the temple, and over the sea toward the mainland.

All over the planet, along coasts and deep lakes, *kahst* were emerging, their mouths gaping, bringing silence to the world.

And all over the planet, before the advance of the *kahst,* Antimovians were disappearing.

Sitting in a deserted square in Pucca, their hands shackled together, Ormbretto and Pierro watched in speechless amazement as their captors suddenly turned away from them, buzzing and beeping at one another in agitation.

Then the wall of silence hit, and they vanished like a ghostly apparition at sunrise: their bodies faded, became indistinct, while around and through them the stones of the street and the plaster sides of buildings were brought into sharp focus. For a moment they were an outline of negative space, held only in the memory of those who saw them, and then they were gone completely.

The machine descended slowly, falling sedately down through the *Torre Vecchio*. Alister, as was his nature, began to worry immediately about the climb back up. But the machine came to a halt beside the doorway to the tower, and hovered there long enough for them to disembark.

Professor Odd was the last to leave; she was peering at an inscription that ran along the ring's edge, and copying it down with one of Alister's pens on her forearm. The machine gave a meaningful tremble. With a sigh the Professor left off her scribbling, and stepped regretfully onto the stone stair.

As soon as it was vacated, the machine dropped like a stone. Down, down, down, until it splashed into unseen water and was gone.

Professor Odd, Elo, Alister and Aleandro exited the tower to find themselves in a tumult of cheering robed Neätans, who were split between cheering for them, and cheering the distant *kahst,* who were still streaming over their heads and disappearing into the sea.

The Professor looked torn, as if she would have very much liked to have a few words with one of the *kahst,* but none of them so much as glanced at the temple, and soon the last of them had disappeared into the water in a tumult of white waves.

Then *Madre* Roda came barging through the crowd, Stefani and Miagroci in tow, bubbling over in Italian. Aleandro looked staggered at the prospect of translating such a deluge, but Professor Odd answered the Neätan in kind, and once she got over the surprise of it, *Madre* Roda led them to an improvised headquarters in a nearby temple, where Maria Rozione sat in a chair surrounded by monitors, tears streaming down her strange face, as she spoke over a videophone to *Tenente* Ormbretto.

Professor Odd gave a small sigh of relief, and said; "Well, that's all right then."

Maria Rozione wheeled around on them, grinning from ear fringe to ear fringe, and snapped her translator back on.

"Professor Odd," she said happily, "I have been discussing the situation with Ormbretto, and we have decided that, in light of your actions, you deserve any honor or reward it is within our power to give you."

Professor Odd was a little taken aback by this. She mumbled something about *having had help,* and *the kahst.* But then she thought of something.

"You're *too kind,* Rozione, but all I really want—in fact, the very reason we came here at all—was for your excellent *pizza.*" She glanced at Alister and Elo, to see that they agreed. "Yes, three of your best *pizza,* I think, will suit us nicely."

* * *

They were slipping out the gates of Casteveglia, each with a wide, flat, savory-smelling white box in their arms, when they found themselves accosted by Aleandro. He was out of breath, and there was a garland of green flowers draped over his shoulders—a side effect of the celebration that was just gaining steam within the temple.

"You're leaving?" he gasped.

Professor Odd hefted her pizza box. "I have what I came for, your world is safe. Nothing left I can do here." She began to walk down the road, but Aleandro kept pace with her.

"I am not so certain about *safe,*" Aleandro said. "We've lost the machine; the *kahst* took it back and flooded the caverns beneath the *Torre Vecchio.* Whatever will we do if those robots come back?"

"Losing that device may be for the best," Professor Odd said, gently. "It is obvious, now, why the Antimovians feared it . . . but you have to wonder, why did the *kahst* try to bury it in the first place? And how is it they could so easily amplify its signal? They work with vibrations naturally (that is how they can fly, how they create their shields), but vibration *patterns?* They had to *learn* that. How did they learn that? It *bothers* me. It also bothers me that they needed *me* to operate the thing for them."

"Well, the *kahst* don't have *hands,*" Elo pointed out, sparing one of hers from the box she carried to wave it at the Professor.

"The *kahst* were able to levitate that whole thing to the top of the *Torre Vecchio,*" Professor Odd said. "They were able to hear its energy signature from within half a mile of rock. They could have found a way to work it . . . they *should* have done. But they didn't . . . that tells me . . . "

"What?" Alister broke out, impatient with the Professor's vague explanations.

"That the machine was originally built to combat the *kahst,*" she said. "Given its unique ammunition, the only conclusion I can see is that the *kahst* must have come from a different universe themselves."

Aleandro had stopped dead in his tracks at this suggestion. But then he shook his head. "Impossible. The *kahst* were not negatively affected by the signal."

"Which brings us back to their unique skill with molecular vibration re-patterning. The *kahst* must have learned the skill in self-defense, and used it to change *themselves* to fit this world's native pattern. Also, they are *organic*: by now their patterns would be native anyway."

"This goes against *everything* that we know of the *kahst,*" Aleandro protested.

Professor Odd shrugged. "I wouldn't worry about it. Wherever the *kahst* came from, I think it is safe to say they are definitely on *your* side now. Or at least, on the side of *Niatano.*"

Aleandro looked hardly reassured by this, but seeing that he would not get a more satisfactory answer, he repeated his second question: What about the robots?

They continued walking, into a growing night whose darkness was mitigated by the huge green planet that hung above their heads. The road stretched out before them, and Elo trotted ahead, eager to get home.

"When I said the machine would shake them out of this universe, I was choosing my metaphor very carefully," Professor

Odd said. "Think about it: what happens to the bits of dirt and lint that you shake out of a coat or carpet?"

"They fall to the ground . . . because of gravity," Alister couldn't help saying.

"Precisely!" said the Professor. "They fall *down.* Now, not a lot of people know this, but the *multiverse* is stacked . . . not in so simple a way as up and down, but that's the easiest way to describe it. So when shaken out of this universe, the Antimovians fell into the nearest *downhill* universe. And the further down you go through the multiverse, the more *unconventional* they get . . . and the more likely they are to be better equipped to deal with the Antimovians."

They had arrived at the little sheepherder's hut where the Oddity's portal was. Beyond it, beyond where the *kahst's* shield had been, the earth was furrowed, scorched, and still smoking from the actions of the robots. They had indeed been trying to dig their way under, and had gotten pretty far. Elo was waiting by the hut, looking out on the destruction with a somber expression.

Professor Odd marched up to the door and took hold of the handle, but did not open it. She turned back to Aleandro, who was standing in the road looking despondent. "Furthermore," she said cheerfully, "unless you have a *very* rare and special device, moving to a universe *uphill* from you is practically impossible. So, no . . . I think you need not worry; you will not see the Antimovians again. *We,* however," she glanced from Elo to Alister, and grinned. "I'm sure we have not seen the last of them. *Grazie e arrivederci, mio caro Aleandro,*" she added, opening the door and ushering her companions inside. "*Ti vedró di nuovo.*"

Aleandro watched the Professor disappear inside the hut and shut the door behind her. He did not try to follow. He smiled, a little ruefully, and began to walk back towards Casteveglia. There was the pop and bang of distant explosions from within the temple, but these were just the result of fireworks being set off, their sparkling bodies streaking through the dark sky and falling in shimmering trails over the sea.

Inside the Oddity, Alister barely had time to breathe a sigh of relief before he was confronted with a sight that turned his blood cold. Behind him he heard Elo give a sharp gasp as she trod on his heel.

Sitting ominously in the center of the room, in front of the table, was a wide, barrel-shaped robot with a domed head and a patchwork pattern of plating on its front. It gave a little click, a little whir, and then said in a sharp, electronic voice:

"MY PANVIRONMENT SUIT IS COMPLETE. WHAT DO YOU THINK OF IT?"

As soon as it spoke all the little incongruities jumped out at Alister. He saw that, unlike the Antimovians, this robot's body was not tapered at the bottom, but was a straight barrel shape. It was girted by a gear, not unlike the tread of a tractor, and its domed head was smooth and appeared to be made of glass—or some other hard, transparent surface. It reflected in a deep blue all the twinkling lights of the Oddity, and around its base was a brass band with ten circular valves. As he watched, one of these opened, and a long, metal-plated tentacle emerged. It waved. A great orange and yellow pinwheel eye pressed itself against the interior of the dome, and blinked at them.

"Hallo Dave!" called the Professor, pushing her way past the gobsmacked Alister and Elo. "You look smashing. Marvelous. *Dressed to kill.*" She winked at them. "We brought pizza back, would you like some?"

"YOU WERE ABSENT LONGER THAN I CALCULATED," Dave said. "WHAT HAPPENED?"

"Funny you should ask that," Elo said, eyeing the panvironment suit warily. But Professor Odd was not disturbed in the slightest by the uncanny resemblance. She swept over and deposited her pizza box on the table. Taking a slice, trailing a string of melted cheese, she pulled up a chair and began to tell Dave all about their adventure.

THE END

NOTES AND ACKNOWLEDGEMENTS

The idea of a world orbiting a red dwarf is not something I invented. The exact circumstances are, of course, imagined, but they were inspired by the very real Gliese 581 system, located about 20 lightyears from our own. Gliese 581 is a red dwarf star with many planets, some of which very nearly fall into the "habitable zone" which could supposedly support life.

I would like to thank the scientists and engineers involved with the Kepler spacecraft project, which has discovered many more extrasolar planets. Reading about these discoveries, and about our own neighbor Jupiter, gave me the idea of a moon-world orbiting a gas giant.

Finally I wish to extend my heartfelt thanks to Anna and Mario Marchi, for their help in fixing up my clumsy Italian.

Vai Umanitá!

—GO

FURTHER READING

This is the second novella of Professor Odd. The next adventure can be found in:

PROFESSOR ODD #3:

THE PROMETHEAN PREDICAMENT

ABOUT THE AUTHOR

Goldeen Ogawa is a writer, illustrator, and cartoonist. She lives in California where she writes stories, draws pictures, and takes care of various animals. She has always loved astronomy, paleontology, and science in general, but found making up stories was more fun. She hopes her stories will inspire other people to do real science, such as astronomy and paleontology.

She is not Italian, but she likes Italy very much.

Her official site and blog is *goldeenogawa.com*.

TEXT AND DESIGN

The body of this book was typeset using LaTeX in Carter Sans, available from *www.linotype.com.*

Cover art and book design by the author.

Made in the USA
Monee, IL
19 September 2024